Illustrated By: Manny Quilop

Published By:
Michelle Hill

Scrappy is so excited that you are coming along to help with our community clean up adventures! Please share with us a little bit about yourself.

ALL ABOUT ME

My Name is : _____

Age : _____

Today's Date: _____

Hi friends, my name is Scrappy, and I'm rounding up friends to help pick-up trash in our city.

Help Scrappy find his way to reach the trash can.

Let's start by washing our truck and making sure our trash cans are clean so it will hold all our trash.

Scrappy is making lots of different faces. Look at the pictures below and see if you can figure out if Scrappy is happy, sad, amazed, silly, angry or crying!

FUNNY FACES

1. _____

2. _____

3. _____

4. _____

5. _____

6. _____

We will need some supplies like garbage bags, and trash cans,

gloves, a broom and a dustpan.

Connect the dot and color me.

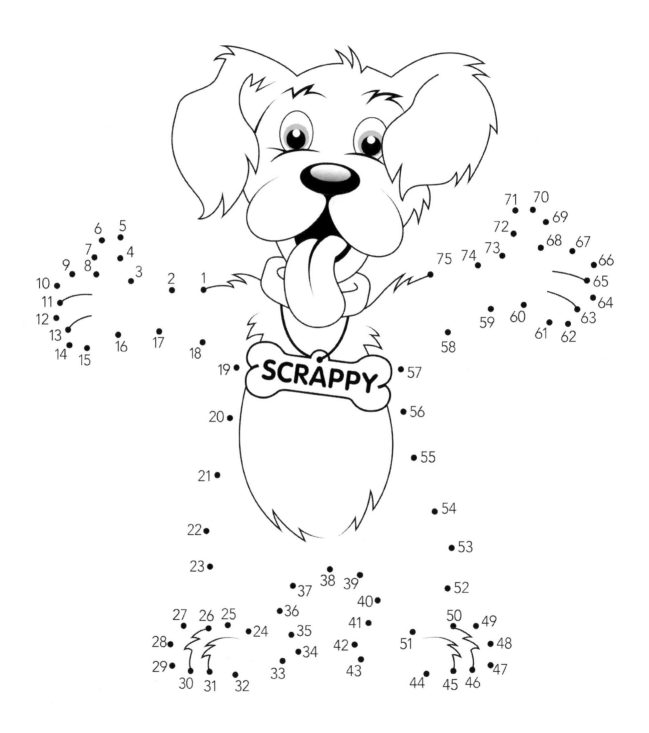

Scrappy and Bella are making similar faces! Draw a line connecting the similar faces that match.

All our friends are here with us and we have our clean-up supplies, lets get started at the city park.

There are so many things to do at the city park!. Draw a picture of your favorite thing to do at your park.

Finish the drawing of Scrappy.

FINISH THE PICTURE!

SCRAPPY

Scrappy is going to need your help. He doesn't know what is trash and what can be recycled.

Help Scrappy separate the trash and recyclables. Color all the trash one color and color all the recyclables a different color.

Next, Let's go to our lake called Silly Dog and start cleaning our lake up.

Scrappy loves playing in the water, he is such a silly dog. Draw a picture of your favorite place to play in the water.

Using the grid as a guide, draw a picture of SCRAPPY in the box below

SCRAPPY DRAW

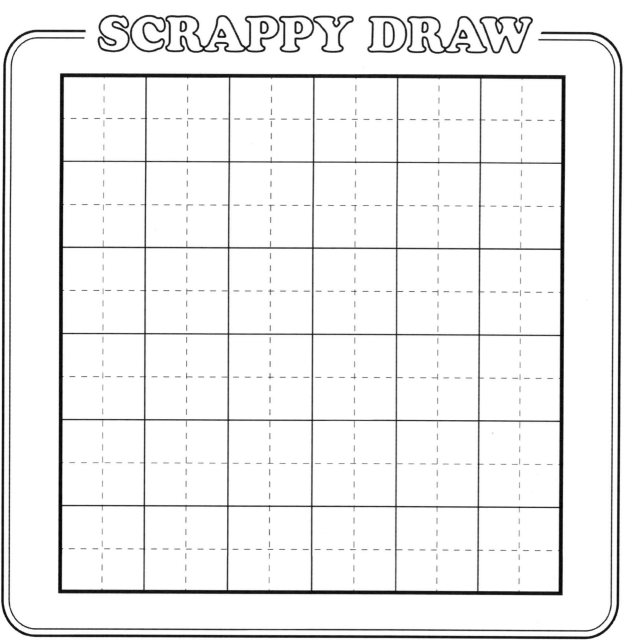

We got our city park and our lake Silly Dog cleaned up. Let's head downtown and clean-up around our houses.

Look at the four pictures. Two of them are exactly alike. Can you find them?

WHICH 2 ARE EXACTLY THE SAME

1.

2.

3.

4.

SCRAPPY

SCRAPPY

SCRAPPY

SCRAPPY

Yeah! Happy Dog Town is clean and we are ready to play. Thank you friends. We couldn't do it without you!

It's Playtime! what is your favorite things to do?

Play on the swings
Slide down the slide
Catch the ball

Write down what is your favorite

_____

Only one of the puzzle pieces below will fit. Can you find the missing piece and complete the puzzle?

Which piece is MISSING?

A.

B.

C.

Made in the USA
Las Vegas, NV
31 October 2022

58527544R00015